The Secrets of the Shipwreck

Contents

Written by Sally Cole
Illustrated by Colin Dowden

Shipwreck

Many Years Ago...

The storm roared around them. Waves swept the doomed ship, lifting it higher onto the reef. The ship creaked and groaned like a large animal in pain. Rain lashed the people on board, stinging their bare skin.

Once more, the ship shuddered and sank lower in the water. Bobbie held his mother's hand tightly as the deck tilted beneath their feet. They slid.

Way down below, the lifeboat looked tiny. It bounced on the huge waves. The rope ladder swayed and banged against the side of the ship.

"Come on, Mary. You must try," Bobbie's father pleaded with his wife.

The ship gave a sudden jerk as it tilted even more sharply into the water. People were screaming and crying. A wave crashed over the top of one of the lifeboats. Frantically, people tried to hold on, fighting for their lives. The waves swept some of them away to drown. The sea threw others onto the jagged rocks, the force of the waves breaking their bones like matchsticks.

"I'll go first!" Bobbie yelled to his mother. "You follow."

Bobbie struggled to hold on to the twisting rope. His hands were shaking and his legs were trembling. At last he reached the lifeboat. Many hands reached out to hold him as he flopped down into the bottom of the boat.

His mother was halfway down the ladder. Her skirt kept twisting around her legs. Suddenly she slipped, tumbled, and crashed into the lifeboat.

"Oh! Are you all right?" Bobbie cried out.

His mother's long hair covered her face and blood streamed from a cut on her head. She hugged Bobbie and said, "Yes, love, I'm all right. But where's your father?"

They looked up. Bobbie's father was climbing down the ladder, which was banging against the side of the ship.

"Can't take any more. Boat's full!" yelled a sailor as he let go of the bottom of the ladder.

"Robert! Robert!" screamed Bobbie's mother.

With the bottom of the ladder flapping around, it was harder than ever to stay on it. Robert was thrown hard against the side of the ship.

"Jump, Dad!" yelled Bobbie.

The men at the oars of the lifeboat were rowing frantically, trying to get away from the sinking ship. They knew that if they stayed too close to the ship as it sank, their lifeboat would get sucked under the waves with it.

Robert pushed out hard as he jumped away from the side of the boat, aiming as close to the moving lifeboat as he could. He swam as fast as he could, but his heavy clothing made him slow. Waves broke over his head. He was swallowing water. He was sinking, drowning.

"Come on, Dad! Keep trying!" yelled Bobbie.

"Please, please wait for him," pleaded Bobbie's mother in desperation.

"Lady, I told you. We've got no more room!" snarled the sailor.

The waves swept them on, leaving Robert behind. As the rain slashed across the sea, they lost sight of him completely.

Bobbie yelled at the sailor, "Stop! Wait!"

"Shut up! Or I'll chuck you over the side, too!" snapped the sailor.

Bobbie lashed out. He kicked and punched the sailor, who hit the boy hard, knocking him sideways. Bobbie's head hit the side of the boat with a thump and he fell unconscious into his mother's arms.

"Bully! Look what you've done!" yelled Bobbie's mother angrily.

"Listen, lady. I've had about enough of you. Any more and you'll both be swimming!" the sailor spat.

Mary wept as she held her son tightly. She knew that the wreck had taken their beloved husband and father from them forever.

Next morning, only the tips of the ship's masts and the sharp teeth of the killer rocks poked out of the water. There were no other survivors.

The lifeboat, with 11 survivors including Bobbie and his mother, drifted out to sea for five days before they were rescued by a passing ship and taken ashore.

A Thirteenth Birthday for Two

Bob leaned over the side of the rubber dinghy. The outboard motor idled, keeping the boat in position. He watched the silver stream of tiny bubbles pop to the surface. Through the clear water he saw a diver kicking his flippers, slowly rising up to the boat.

Maria said, "Looks as if he's got something. His bag looks pretty heavy."

"Yeah," Bob, her brother, said. "This is where we got that big haul of clams last time."

Their father's head popped out of the water. He spat the mouthpiece to his regulator out of his mouth and said, "Good haul today. There's plenty to share."

Bob took hold of the bag and Maria helped him to lift it into the boat. It was very heavy.

"Wow! They're big ones, Dad!" said Maria.

Rob Angelo climbed into the boat, followed a few moments later by his good friend, Jerry. They pulled their masks off, shrugged their dive tanks from their shoulders, and kicked off their flippers.

"The water was so clear we found them easily," Rob said cheerfully.

"Yeah. Must be our best haul yet," added Jerry.

But Bob had other things on his mind. "When can we start our diving course, Dad?" he said.

"Yeah, you said we could when we turned 13, and we'll be 13 tomorrow," added Maria.

"Don't I know it!" laughed their father. "You've been going on about it for weeks! You'll just have to wait and see what happens tomorrow."

The boat skimmed across the water to the boat ramp. They loaded it onto the trailer and headed for home.

The next morning the twins were up very early. They raced into their dad's room. Dad lay in bed, pretending to snore. The harder they shook him, the more deeply asleep he seemed. In the end, Maria and Bob tickled his feet and that finally did the trick. Dad jumped from the bed and chased them, screaming with laughter, into the kitchen.

"OK, you two! Happy birthday! Now come with me," he said.

Dad led them out to the garage, lifted the cover off the boat, and said, "Look inside."

Maria and Bob scrambled quickly up onto the trailer and leaned into the boat. What they saw inside delighted them.

"Wow! Dad, that is so cool!" said Bob.

Maria hugged their dad. "Thank you, thank you, Dad," she said.

Inside the dinghy were two wet suits, two sets of flippers, and two buoyancy compensators, as well as tanks, regulators, and masks. It was everything they'd need to start diving.

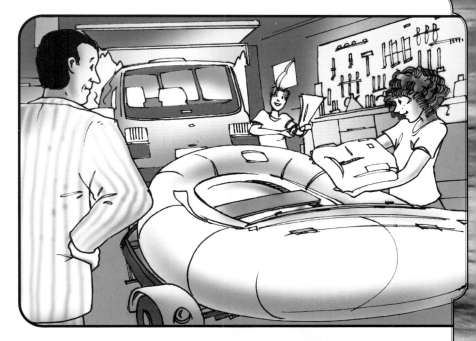

"I figured if you're going to learn to dive, you might as well do it properly," said Dad. "Your first lesson is this afternoon, so you'd better hurry up. You both need a medical certificate from the doctor to say that you're fit. So move it! We have an appointment in an hour."

Let the Diving Begin!

A smiley woman appeared and said, "Hi, I'm Josie. I'm here to teach you how to dive. It's fun. And when you know the right way to do it, you'll have no problems."

Over the next few weeks, Bob and Maria learned to dive. They learned how to put on their gear, how to use it, and how to care for it. First they studied in the classroom, then in the pool, and last of all in the sea.

The twins learned what happens to the air inside your body when you dive. When air is trapped in the lungs, ears, or stomach, it is compressed as you dive. If divers hold their breath while ascending, air inside their lungs will expand, causing the lungs to burst. So, they learned to never hold their breath while underwater.

"There's so much to learn," said Maria.

"I didn't realize how much you need to know before you can even get into the water," said Bob.

"Diving is one of the most dangerous sports you can do," said their father. "That's why you must always know exactly what to do, in any situation. And never, never panic."

"I guess we're pretty lucky having each other," said Maria, looking at Bob. "The instructor told us never to dive alone, but always with a buddy. Bob's always been my buddy anyway."

Bob grinned, gave her a shove, and said, "You're not too bad, for a sister!"

As the lessons continued, the twins learned the proper way to prepare for a dive. They learned how to behave when underwater. They learned the proper hand signals that are the diver's language, and how to show if they were out of air, needed help, or were simply OK.

At last, it was time for their first deep-sea dive. The twins were very excited.

The Marine Sanctuary

"Next lesson will be at the Marine Sanctuary," the instructor said. "There are lots of beautiful fish. Some are really huge. They've been protected for a long time," she continued, "so some are 50 to 60 years old. They are quite tame and will swim close to you. Just don't make any sudden movements."

The twins raced home to tell their father. They burst through the door shouting, "Dad! Dad! Tomorrow we're doing our deep-sea dive!"

"We're going right out to the Marine Sanctuary," said Bob excitedly.

"It'll be so cool," said Maria.

The day of the dive, the twins were up and ready early. They could hardly wait to be in the water.

"Good luck," said Dad, giving them both a hug, "I'll be waiting to hear all about it."

They loaded the dive bottles and the rest of their gear into the boat. Then they headed out to the Marine Sanctuary island, way out in the bay. In the distance, they could see the sea breaking roughly over sharp jagged rocks.

"Looks like a reef. The island must be part of it," said Maria, pointing.

"They say that a ship was wrecked on those rocks a long time ago," said the instructor. "There was a terrible storm and the boat went down quickly."

"That would've been scary," said Maria. "I wonder if anyone was drowned."

"Maybe the wreck's still there," said Bob. "Maybe people can dive down to it."

"Come on," said the instructor, "enough talk. It's time to see how good you are."

The water was warm and clear. Huge fish peered at the divers as they swished gracefully past. They saw the eyes of lobsters watching from the rocks where they hid as the divers swam past. Tiny fish darted in and out of the kelp as it swayed gently back and forth in the current. They saw a garden of beautiful underwater plants.

After 20 minutes, the instructor gave the thumbs up sign to go back to the surface. Gently, they moved their flippers, slowly rising to the surface.

"That was amazing!" said Bob, spitting his mouthpiece out and pulling off his mask.

"Good dive, kids. I'm really pleased with you," said the instructor, smiling.

"It was so quiet and peaceful down there," said Maria, "I can't wait to go down again."

"It was just the way Dad described it," said Bob, "so beautiful and so calm. I wish we could stay down there forever!"

Their father was waiting for them when they returned to the beach.

"I thought I'd meet you here. I couldn't wait to hear how it all went," he said.

"It was absolutely amazing," said Bob.

"Sure was," said Maria.

"We saw some huge fish and our instructor was telling us about the reef out there," said Bob. "She said a ship was wrecked on it a long time ago."

"I wonder what the ship was called and who was on it," said Maria.

The Tale of the Shipwreck

Dad looked thoughtful. He sat down on the sand and said, "Sit here beside me, both of you. I have a story to tell you."

When they were sitting next to him, Dad said, "A long long time ago, your great-grandparents decided to immigrate to this country. They wanted to start a new life. Your great-grandfather, Robert Angelo, set out with his wife, Mary, and Bobbie, their ten-year-old son.

They had almost reached the end of their voyage when a terrible storm struck. The ship was blown onto a reef and wrecked. Only 11 people survived the wreck. Your great-grandmother and her son were two of them. Your great-grandfather was drowned."

"Wow! Dad, we never knew that!" said Bob. "Why did you never tell us?"

"Yeah, why didn't you tell us before?" said Maria. "It's so sad."

"Well, the ten-year-old boy was my father, your grandfather," said Dad. "He never wanted to talk about it. The memories were too painful. But now that he is dead and no longer with us, the story can finally be told."

"Was that the ship wrecked on the reef out there?" asked Maria.

"Yes, Maria, it was," said Dad. "It's very sad, but it happened a long time ago," he continued. "And if they hadn't decided to come to this country, none of us would be here today!"

Bob said, "Dad, can we go out there? Can we dive down to see the wreck?"

"I don't know how much of it will be left after all this time," Dad replied. "But I guess we could go and look, maybe next weekend. Let's just wait and see how the weather is."

"Great!" said Maria. "It'll be so exciting!"

"Yes!" said Bob.

Dive, Dive, Dive

The twins could hardly wait until the weekend. On Saturday morning, the sea was calm. It looked like a good day for a dive. They loaded all the gear into the boat and motored out to the reef.

It looked quite harmless with the waves gently breaking over it, but they knew how dangerous it really was. And somewhere, in those waters, their great-grandfather's life had ended.

Dad swung the boat away from the reef and they cruised along slowly. Bob put on his mask and snorkel and leaned over the side, his face in the water.

"It's so clear. I can see the sandy bottom," he said.

Maria leaned over the other side of the boat and looked down through the water.

"There's something sticking up out of the sand. It looks like a bit of wood," she said.

"Maybe it's part of the wreck," said Bob.

"OK. We'll drop the anchor here," said Dad. "Then we'll explore. Bob, you get the *Diver down* flag ready, then you and I will dive while Maria keeps an eye on the boat," said Dad. "Don't worry, Maria, you and I will dive after Bob and I come up."

As soon as Dad and Bob had their scuba gear on, they started their descent. Gently, they moved their flippers. Smoothly they slid through the water.

Down, down, down they went. Below, a dark shape lay, resting on the seabed. Seaweed waved from the holes in its sides. Tiny fish darted in and out. It was the wreck.

Bob swam to a round hole. Maybe it was once a porthole. He peered into the gloom inside.

Suddenly, a twisting yellow body shot from the hole. Its wide mouth and snapping jaws missed Bob's hand by a fraction. Bob jumped back, frantically kicking his legs.

Dad grabbed Bob's leg and shook his head, making Bob understand he must not shoot to the surface. He must never panic. Together, the two of them slowly kicked their way back up to the boat.

The boat was just as they had left it but the weather had changed. Storm clouds banked on the shoreline. The land was vanishing behind a rain squall. A strong wind was blowing from the land, out into the bay.

"You OK, son? That was pretty scary," said Dad.

"What was that thing?" asked Bob.

"That was a moray eel. They can grow quite big," said Dad. "I'd say that one was longer than you. Their jaws are incredibly powerful. Lucky it missed your hand or you could be missing a couple of fingers!"

Stormy Weather – A Big Swim

Glancing at the skyline, Dad said, "Time to head for home. Sorry Maria, but I don't like the look of the weather. Let's stow the gear and get the anchor up."

Disappointed, Maria pulled the *Diver down* flag in. She and Bob stowed it and the rest of the gear away.

"Give me a hand with these life jackets," said Bob. "They're caught on the locker door."

Maria pulled the life jackets and suddenly they jerked free. Just then a gust of wind hit the boat, making it lurch. Maria was already off balance. With a cry she fell sideways, hitting her head before tumbling into the sea. She wasn't wearing dive gear or a life jacket!

"Throw her the life buoy!" shouted Dad.

Bob quickly tossed the life buoy into the water.

Despairingly, they watched as the wind and strong current swept it away. Maria was drifting away, too.

"Help me, Dad!" she screamed.

She was having trouble swimming. Her head kept slipping under the water. Water was pouring in through her mouth, into her lungs. She had to breathe! Maria struggled back toward the surface. She had to get there. Stars flashed before her eyes. She felt so dizzy her lungs were ready to burst. She was drowning.

Frantically she kicked again and felt herself rising up through the water. At last her head popped out of the water. She gasped air into her oxygen-starved lungs.

"Dad!" she screamed, as another wave filled her mouth and she sank again. This time, she was much weaker. This time, she sank even deeper.

The boat was tossing and rolling as the wind increased. Waves washed over it. The motor, drowning beneath the water, coughed and died.

Dad yelled, "You keep trying the motor, Bob! I'll go after your sister."

Pulling on a life jacket, Dad jumped into the water. The waves swept him along as he swam after Maria. He could see her drifting out closer to the reef, where the waves were now pounding.

Behind him in the boat, Bob was still trying to restart the motor. It, too, was now being swept out to sea, closer to the reef, the same reef that had already brought tragedy to the Angelo family.

"I wonder if that reef is going to get us, too," thought Bob as he kept desperately trying to start the motor.

Out in the bay, as the waves grew bigger, Rob Angelo finally reached Maria. She was only just breathing. He held her face up out of the water.

"Come on, Maria. You must try," he pleaded, not knowing he was using the same words that his grandfather had used, all those years ago.

Maria's eyes fluttered open. She coughed as her father held her tight.

"I'm OK, Dad," she said.

"That's my girl. Now we've just got to get out of here," he responded.

Mayday, Mayday, Mayday

Back on the boat, Bob was having no luck with the motor. It was time to call for help.

"Mayday, mayday, mayday," Bob called, making the international call for a vessel in distress.

"Coastal rescue receiving. Vessel calling, please identify your position," came the response.

Bob said who and where they were and quickly added, "We're drifting near rocks, in heavy seas! Motor disabled. Two people overboard."

The voice from the coastal rescue boat said, "We're on our way. Keep this radio channel open."

Bob was frantic. He yelled into the microphone, "How long will you be? My dad and sister are drowning out there. They're getting a lot closer to the rocks, and so is the boat!"

"You're doing very well, son," came the comforting voice. "Keep talking to me. We're not far away from you now."

In the water, Dad had managed to grab the life buoy and pull it firmly over Maria's head and arms. He and Maria were still being carried closer to the reef, but not quite as quickly as before. He anxiously watched the boat, with Bob on board, getting closer and closer to the rocks. He could see Bob holding the microphone in his hand and hoped he was calling the coastal rescue service.

Suddenly, emerging from the heavy sheets of rain came the rescue boat. It headed straight to Maria and her father.

Bob's microphone came alive in his hand, "We'll pick up the people in the water first, then try to get a towline over to you. Just hold on, son, not long to go now. You're doing very well," came the comforting voice again.

Bob felt a little better knowing help was at hand. He watched as one of the crew threw a life buoy with a line tied to it. He shouted to Dad, "Put it over your head and we'll pull you in."

The first throw missed, falling short of Dad's stretching arm. He couldn't let go of Maria, because she would float away and drown. Once more the life buoy flew through the air. This time it landed close enough. Dad grabbed it and pulled it over his head.

Carefully, the rescue crew pulled the line in. Once Maria and her dad were pulled to the stern of the boat, many hands lifted them, first the half-drowned girl and then her father, to the safety of the boat. Quickly, they were wrapped in thermal blankets as the coastal rescue boat headed for Bob.

By this time, the huge rocks were uncomfortably close to the small boat. Bob could feel the uncontrollable panic rising in him.

"We'll have to throw a line to him. Do you think he'll be able to tie it on?" one of the rescue crew asked Dad.

Dad answered, "He's good on a boat, but it's a lot to expect in these heavy seas."

"We'll have to see if we can get the towline across anyway, or we could lose both Bob and the boat," said the man.

A crew member steered the boat around so that it was close enough to throw the line.

"Ready, Bob," he yelled.

"OK," the shout came back over the sound of the roaring sea.

Bob braced himself against the side of the tossing boat. The wind blew stinging salt spray into his eyes, blinding him. The rope came snaking across. Bob grabbed at it. He missed, but luckily as the rope slid away the loop in the end of it caught on a post. Thinking quickly, Bob ran to the bow of the boat and tied the rope. Carefully, he made his way back to the cabin. From there, he watched as the coastal rescue boat slowly moved away, towing the smaller boat behind it.

Rob Angelo turned to the crew of the rescue boat and said, "I can't thank you enough. You've saved all our lives, as well as the boat. For a while I thought that reef was going to be the end of us, too."

"What do you mean? Has someone you know already died on the reef?" asked a crew member.

"My grandfather lost his life in a shipwreck there," replied Dad.

"It doesn't seem to be a good place for you or your family," replied the crew member.

Dad hugged Maria and said, "You're right. I think we'll avoid this spot from now on!"

A Strange Coincidence

Three Days Later...

"Dad, guess what I found out while I was at the library today?" asked Maria.

Dad smiled and said, "I imagine you're probably going to tell me anyway, aren't you? It's not like you to keep something interesting to yourself."

"Well," said Maria, "I was searching through some books for information on the shipwreck and I found out that the ship was named the *Mary Rose*."

"Is that why you called our boat *Maria Rose*, Dad?" asked Bob.

"No," replied Dad, with a smile.

"Why then, Dad?" asked Maria.

"I named it after you, Maria," replied Dad, "and after your great-grandmother, Mary Rose. I didn't even know the name of the ship that was wrecked. This is the first I've heard of it."

The twins looked at each other and shivered. It seemed like one too many coincidences.